Friends Are Forever

Jump over the Puddle

Written by Emma Quay

Illustrated by Anna Walker

SCHOLASTIC

For Zane ~ EQ

For Jack, Tom and Alice ~ AW

First published in 2009 by Scholastic Australia

This edition first published in 2010 by Scholastic Children's Books

Euston House, 24 Eversholt Street

London NW1 1DB

a division of Scholastic Ltd

www.scholastic.co.uk

London ~ New York ~ Toronto ~ Sydney ~ Auckland

Mexico City ~ New Delhi ~ Hong Kong

www.emmaquay.com

www.annawalker.com.au

ISBN 978 1407 12078 2

Hello, Panda.

Hello, Sheep.

Hello, Owl.

All together . . . friends are forever.

Panda, Owl and Sheep
find a puddle.

"Jump over the puddle," says Panda.

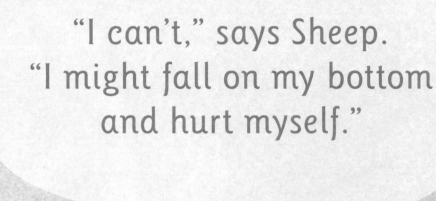

"I can't," says Sheep.
"I might fall on my bottom
and hurt myself."

"Jump over the puddle," says Owl.

"I can't,"
says Sheep.

and she falls . . .

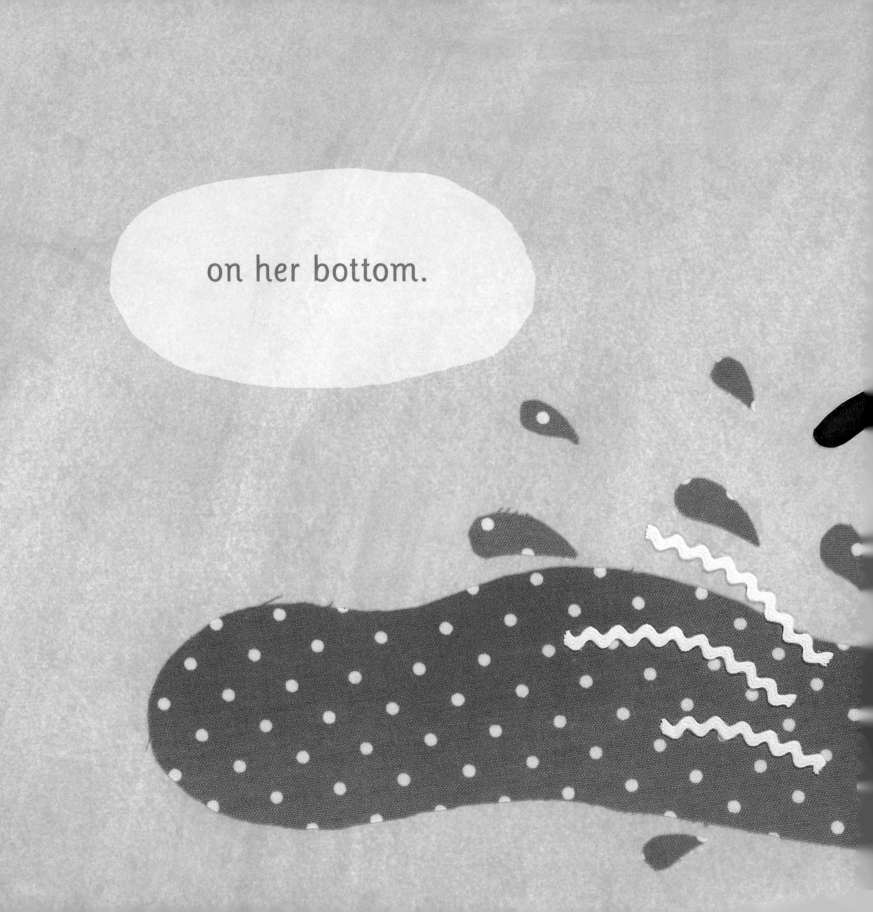